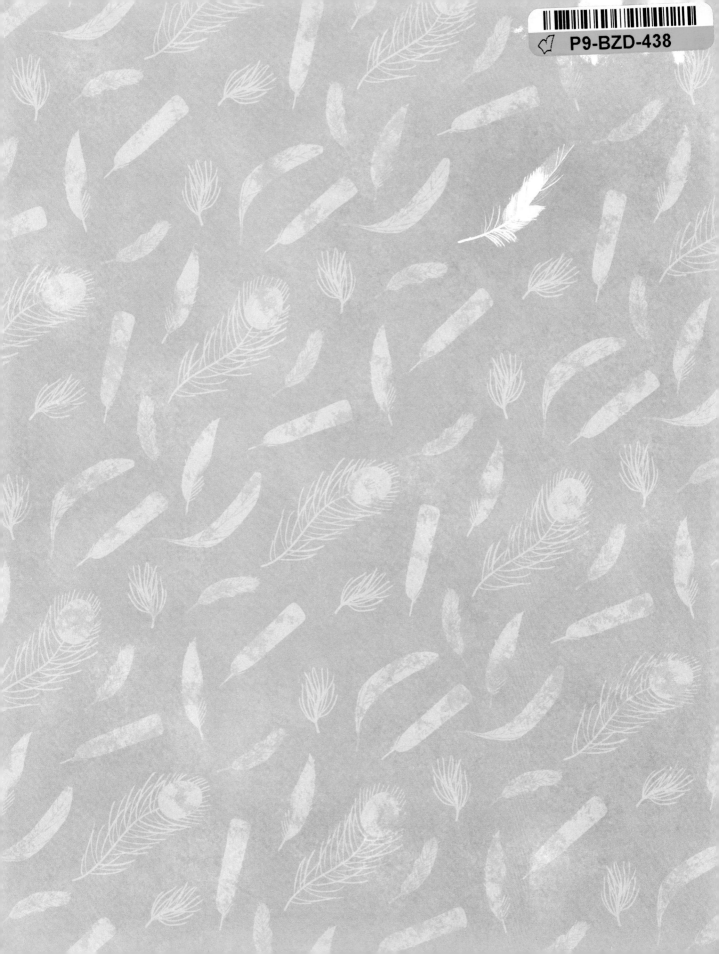

To SMZ, for never saying no and Kathy Landwehr, for saying yes, again. Thank you! —F. Z.

For Seth, always —S. F. C.

Published by
Peachtree Publishing Company Inc.
1700 Chattahoochee Avenue
Atlanta, Georgia 30318-2112
*www.peachtree-online.com*

Text © 2020 by Farhana Zia
Illustrations © 2020 by Stephanie Fizer Coleman

Edited by Kathy Landwehr
Design and composition by Nicola Simmons Carmack and Adela Pons
The illustrations were rendered digitally.

Printed in November 2019 by Tien Wah Press in Malaysia
10 9 8 7 6 5 4 3 2 1
First Edition
ISBN 978-1-68263-129-4

Library of Congress Cataloging-in-Publication Data

Names: Zia, F. (Farhana), author. | Coleman, Stephanie Fizer, illustrator.
Title: Lali's feather / written by Farhana Zia ; illustrated by Stephanie Fizer Coleman.
Description: First edition. | Atlanta, Georgia : Peachtree Publishing Company Inc., [2020] | Summary: "Lali finds a feather in the field. Is little feather lost? Lali sets out to find feather a home"— Provided by publisher.
Identifiers: LCCN 2019019054 | ISBN 9781682631294
Subjects: | CYAC: Feathers—Fiction. | Lost and found possessions—Fiction.
Classification: LCC PZ7.Z482 Lal 2020 | DDC [E]—dc23 LC record available at *https://lccn.loc.gov/2019019054*

# Lali's
## FEATHER

Written by **Farhana Zia**

Illustrated by **Stephanie Fizer Coleman**

PEACHTREE
ATLANTA

Lali found a feather in the field.

Whose feather? She did not know.

It was a sweet feather, though.

*Oo ma!* Was little feather lost? Lali

set out to find feather a home.

"Rooster, Rooster! Is this feather yours?"
Lali asked.

"*Na*, Lali, *na!*" Rooster replied. "My
feather is a big feather. It makes me a
lordly bird. That feather is a little feather.
It's not mine!"

"Crow, Crow! Is this feather
yours?" Lali asked.

"*Na*, Lali, *na!*" Crow replied. "My feather is a perky
feather. It makes me a speedy bird. That feather is a
pokey feather. It's not mine!"

"Peacock, Peacock! Is this feather yours?" Lali asked.

"*Na*, Lali, *na!*" Peacock replied. "My feather is a fancy feather. It makes me a handsome bird. That feather is a plain feather. It's not mine!"

"Cheeky birds!" cried Lali. "If you don't want feather, I shall keep it."

And that is what she did!

"Feather and I will do one hundred things!" Lali said.

She ran to show Hen her feather.

"Go! Go!" Hen giggled. "My feather can keep
my babies warm. Lali O Lali, what can little
feather do?"

"Feather can do this!" Lali said.

Lali and feather wrote a note to Goat!

"Oo ma!" Hen exclaimed. "I didn't know little feather could do that!"

Lali ran to show Duck her feather.

"Go! Go!" Duck chuckled. "My feather
can keep me dry from shore to shore.
Lali O Lali, what can pokey feather do?"

"Feather can do this!" Lali said.

Feather and Lali swept the floor from door to door!

"*Oo ma!*" Duck cried. "I didn't know pokey feather
could do that!"

Lali ran to show Blue Jay her feather.

"Go! Go!" Blue Jay tittered. "My feather makes everyone say *ooo* and *aah*. Lali O Lali, what can plain feather do?"

"Feather can do this!" said Lali. Feather and Lali fanned the fire a little higher.

"*Oo ma!*" Blue Jay cried. "I didn't know plain feather could do all that!"

Feather and Lali made sister sneeze.

Feather and Lali tickled Bapu's toes too!

Little feather twirled and whirled. It shimmered and glimmered!

"*Wah!* It's a clever feather!" observed the birds.

Then big old wind burst with a whoosh and

gave little feather a great big lift!

Feather flip-flopped, teetered-tottered!

Up went feather. Up...up...higher...higher...

Over the huts, over smelly bins, over

mango tree and tamarind tree!

*Oi* feather, stop!

Feather didn't stop!

Feather flitted...

Feather fluttered...

Feather floated away!

*Oo ma!*

"Feather, sweet feather!" sobbed Lali.

Rooster wept too.

"Lali, dear Lali, you can have my feather!" cried Hen.
"It cannot write a note, but it's a warm feather!"

"Do take mine!" cried Duck. "It cannot sweep a floor,
but it's a dry feather!"

"Here's mine!" cried Blue Jay. "It cannot fan a fire but
it's a colorful feather!"

But Lali didn't want their feathers. Lali
wanted her feather…her little, pokey,
plain feather.

"Lali, dear Lali, dry your tears!" Crow cried. "I will bring sweet feather back in a jiffy, in a snap, in the blink of an eye!"

Crow flapped her speedy feathers and flew from tree to tree.

And Peacock? Why, he also flew, because he missed feather too!

Fly, birds, fly! Faster! Faster!

Wait, feather, wait, *na!*

*Jai Ho!* Lali's feather came back!

"Hip hip hurray!" cried the birds. "Lali O Lali! We want to play with feather too!"

Lali and feather played in the field with friends until the end of the day.

The next day, Lali found a button in the field. Whose button? She did not know. It was a shiny button though!